Ohio Reading Circle
1979   7th

TO WALK ON TWO FEET

TO WALK
ON TWO FEET

by
MARJORIE COOK

THE WESTMINSTER PRESS
Philadelphia

Book Design by Dorothy Alden Smith

First edition

Published by The Westminster Press ®
Philadelphia, Pennsylvania

PRINTED IN THE UNITED STATES OF AMERICA
9 8 7 6 5 4 3 2 1

ACKNOWLEDGMENTS
For their help and advice, the author wishes to thank
    Mrs. Pat Hull—School Nurse, Fife School District, Fife, Washington

    Mr. Lenart Ceder—Tacoma Limb and Brace Co., 8th and K, Tacoma,
    Washington

    Good Samaritan Hospital, Puyallup, Washington—Rehabilitation Cen-
    ter

For background information, the author is indebted to
    Morrissey, Alice B., *Rehabilitation Nursing*. G. P. Putnam's Sons, Inc.,
    1951

Library of Congress Cataloging in Publication Data

Cook, Marjorie, 1920–
    To walk on two feet.

    SUMMARY: Following an automobile accident in which
she lost both legs below her knees, Carrie identifies
a burglar. Subsequently she receives threats to keep
silent, and finally her life is in danger.
    [Physically handicapped—Fiction] I. Title.
PZ7.C7713To   [Fic]   77–17369
ISBN 0–664–32628–5

1

THE MOMENTS OF WAKING WERE ALWAYS DIFFICULT. YOU began to feel and everything was real again. Sleep was the only escape and it never lasted long enough. Even that could be ruined by the dream of crashing metal, screams, dripping blood, and overpowering pain.

"Carrie." Mother's voice was just a whisper.

"H'mm?" Better not ignore her.

"Honey, Grandma and Grandpa Karns are here. Dinnertime soon. May I help you get ready? Daddy will be up to carry you downstairs in a few minutes. Here is your new robe."

"No. Leave me alone."

"Wake up, dear. Of course you are going down for your birthday dinner. Doctor Blain said it would be wonderful for you. Everyone has special surprises. We are so glad to have you home."

Mother certainly did bustle at times, especially when she was nervous. So it was Carrie's fifteenth birthday, and she was just home from the hospital after days and weeks. She didn't want to move.

"Carrie. Carrie Karns."

"O.K., O.K., if I have to."

5

She let her mother do everything for her, although she could do it herself if she wanted. She even let her mother comb her hair. How she hated it short. It made her blue eyes seem more staring and her small nose more freckled. Her tan was all gone, too. She just didn't look like herself.

"Now, Honey, you rest a bit. I'll send Daddy for you when we're ready. If the pain bothers you, be sure to signal me. We'll tuck you in again." She gave Carrie a quick kiss as she left.

The pain. It really was almost gone unless she moved suddenly or stretched too hard. She had learned that you get more sympathy if you look as if it hurts.

Carrie glanced around her room. She hated the way it was changed. It had been so cozy before, with all her things just the way she wanted them. Now everything was moved. It just wasn't the way she had expected it after her long absence.

But the family had been excited and pleased when they showed it so proudly. It was on the upstairs front corner of the house and they had put in two large windows on each side. The drapes were tan with gold threads in a pattern, meeting at the corner where a glass-fronted cupboard held her doll and horse collections.

The new carpet was pale gold, and the dresser, bookcase, and other furnishings were cherry, a lovely reddish brown. Even the bed was different. It was higher, with a plain cherry headboard. There was a deep-blue woven spread that matched an upholstered love seat. Her old wooden rocker was now blue with gold cushions. There were many pillows and new lamps. A gold one with an adjustable chain was within reach at the head of the bed.

Mother had explained that they had made her room more like a studio since she would want her friends to visit here. They had tried to make it nice for her. It must have cost a lot.

But then, there must be insurance money, gobs of it.

"Sis"—Toby was standing in the doorway—"can I come in? Mom said I always have to ask."

She hadn't seen her little brother for weeks. He looked a little taller. "Sure, come on."

He came and stood by the bed, deliberately keeping his eyes on her face. His freckles stood out and his hair was the usual disordered straw-colored mop.

"I like your hair short. Glad you're home. Carrie, can I see? Please?"

"There's nothing to see."

"That's what I want to see—nothin'!"

They both looked down where her lower legs and feet should make bumps under the covers. It looked strange to see nothing but smoothness. Toby's eyes were huge in his chubby face when he looked back at her.

"Go away. Get out. Don't ever come back!" Carrie screamed at him.

He scuttled away and almost bumped into Daddy in the doorway.

"What's wrong here?" he asked. "Toby bother you? He had strict orders."

"It's O.K."

"Happy birthday, Honey. You are such a lovely load." He lifted her carefully, hugging her to him.

She felt warm and safe as he carried her gently and tucked her in the wheelchair at the foot of the stairs. Her red velvet robe was new and soft, and he put a white lacy shawl over her knees.

"Let me give you my special gift now." He took a small jeweler's box from his pocket.

She popped it open. There was a lovely gold filigree ring with a sparkling ice-blue stone. He slipped it on her ring finger and gave it a kiss.

"Every time you feel low, Sweetie, remember I love you."

"Thank you, Daddy," she said. Her tears were close again.

2

"CARRIE, DO YOU PLAN TO SLEEP ALL DAY?" HER MOTHER'S gentle voice said, as she opened the side drapes. "It's almost noon, Sweetie. There are things to see and do. You wake up while I bring up your tray."

The protective blackness of drugged sleep had been warm and deep. It was a long way to climb back to reality. No dream! She hadn't had the dream. There was bright sunshine in her face.

Without moving, she opened her eyes. The side yard looked golden. The large maple glowed with its new bright-green leaves. She pushed herself up and leaned on one arm. Lilacs were in bloom. She could almost smell them.

The curtains moved in an upstairs window next door across the yard. Someone was looking at her. She made an ugly face. She hoped Mrs. Riley could see. Mrs. Riley had no right to stare. Carrie flopped back down. Then she heard voices.

"Yeah, she's awake. But we can't go in." It was Toby's voice in the hall. "I gotta have permission."

"But you promised." It was that stupid little Riley girl from next door. The stage whispers carried.

"Can't help it," Toby said.

9

"You call her then. I gave you my candy bar. You promised I could see her no legs."

"Mother," Carrie screamed. "Mother."

She heard the kids run down the front stairs as her mother came up the back. "What is it?" she asked anxiously.

"Does everyone have to look at me?"

"What do you mean? There is no one here."

"Oh, no? There is Mrs. Riley." She pointed and the curtain plainly fluttered. "Toby and Sara were in the hall. I don't want to see anyone."

"Now, Carrie, you know how anxious everyone is to see you up."

"Up? You know I can't get up."

"Of course you can. The wheelchair will take you anywhere."

"Not downstairs."

"Even that. Daddy has priced a chair elevator. When you need it, we will get it."

"Oh."

"The sooner you get around, the sooner you can begin to learn to walk."

"I can't. I won't use that chair. Not ever."

"Now listen, young lady, you are extremely fortunate to be alive. You have every chance to be completely well. You are strong and intelligent. You have many people who love you and will help you. You are not going to act this way."

"I'll lie right here and rot. I won't get up and I won't be stared at. I'll go sell pencils on the street corner. I won't do anything!"

"And I won't come in this room unless you can be pleasant."

Her mother put a little gold bell on the table by the bed and went quietly out.

Carrie made the ugliest face she could at the window next door. It didn't do any good, because she could see Mrs. Riley coming through the hedge and up the path to the back door with a covered dish in her hand.

They were always heckling her. At the hospital she had been pestered all day—every few minutes. Even in the night they had come in to check and often rebandage. Exercise. Do this. Do that. Exercise.

No wonder she had quit. She had refused to do anything. Then they had let her come home. And she wouldn't ever go back. Not ever.

She twisted the ring on her finger. The blue stone winked "I love you." She turned it inside her hand.

That ugly Sara Riley was climbing the maple tree to look in the window. She could see Toby's anxious face turned up watching her.

She covered up her head. I hate everybody. The whole world is ugly and mean and staring. I'm hungry. My teeth taste all furry. I hurt. No one cares. I can't get up. A hot tear squeezed out and ran down to her nose. It tickled. Even a dumb old tear bothered her. She sniffed. No one had put tissues where she could reach them.

She rolled over and opened the drawer by her bed. It was full of unopened get-well and birthday cards, some pretty notepaper and two new pens.

The second drawer held a box of malted milk balls, her favorite candy. She popped several in her mouth. There was a little box with a pink ribbon. The tiny card was in Grandma's writing: "For my Little Angel. We love you."

She opened it. It was the cutest little doll dressed in a frothy spangled-blue angel costume with silver wings. It had long yellow hair. Tucked in the bottom of the box were several other costumes.

As she sat up she knocked the little bell off the table and it rolled away, tinkling loudly. Mother came in almost at once carrying a covered tray.

"I'm sorry, Mother," Carrie found herself saying, "I guess I need you."

"O.K., Honey. I know."

Soon Carrie was propped up, clean and comfortable. The breakfast-lunch tray looked good. Mother admired Angel and set her on the tray table Grandpa had made to fit over her knees on the bed.

As she ate slowly, she found and pulled out a shallow drawer and saw a whole set of art supplies. Maybe she would draw after she finished eating.

Mother and Toby made several trips into her room, bringing the gifts she had opened the night before. The students and teachers at school had taken a collection and sent a small portable television in a bright-red case.

Her uncles and aunts had gone together and given her a telephone of her own. It would soon be installed. It would also have a buzzer so she could call downstairs.

Her Sunday school class had sent four new books. There was a note on the gift card that gave several telephone numbers to call if she wanted someone to go to the library for her or run other errands.

There was candy, and plants, and flowers, and perfume, and even more she hadn't opened.

Toby helped without saying a word. He had started to put the soft blue plush dog he had given her on the foot of the bed.

He gave her a quick glance and put it on the floor by the window. Then he hurried out.

"Carrie, what is wrong with Toby?" Mother asked.

"I scared him."

"You did? Why?"

"He wanted to see where I had no legs. Sara bribed him. She wanted to see too. I yelled at him." She felt all hot and mad again.

"He is just a curious little boy. This is a unique happening. He is big stuff with the other children because his sister—"

"Yeah."

"There is not much point in being mean to him. He could help you in so many ways. Better think it over."

"Where is Mrs. Riley?"

"She brought you some cookies. I told her you didn't feel well enough to see anyone. However, I won't do that much longer. You have to see people. They are anxious to welcome you home and wish you well. So many have called."

"I won't see anyone."

"The pastor asked if he could come by tomorrow after church."

"No."

"You saw people in the hospital."

"That's different."

"How?"

"It just is."

"Well, here is one thing you will face. The nurse will be by each morning to check your legs until you take care of them yourself. You can, you know. We are mighty lucky this is on her way to work and she offered to do it. And she can't be expected to do it always."

"O.K."

"Also, the school is sending a visiting teacher beginning Monday. They said you could catch up, with a little extra effort, and finish your junior high work. Then you can enter high school in September with your class."

"I can't. You know I can't."

"They think so. I know you can. You can do anything you really want to do. Anything!"

"Oh, Mother!"

It felt so good to cry. She had held it in so long. It was just as if a big balloon inside had suddenly burst.

"Mother, it's just too much. I'll never be able to walk. It's much too hard. And takes too long. And hurts too much!"

"I know, Honey. You have to want to more than anything else in the world."

"Please help me."

"You know I will."

Her mother held her, rocking her gently. She was crying too. Their tears ran together where their cheeks touched.

"We can do it together, Baby," her mother said.

The tears were finally gone. But the closeness would always be there. Mother moved her tray and smoothed the covers.

"Shall I open the other drapes?"

"I guess so."

"I'll close them so you can rest when I come upstairs again." She left quietly.

The view out the front showed a street corner, some more big trees, and an upper corner of the school building. She just looked, not feeling.

She held the angel doll tight in her hand, stroking its long blond hair.

3

"HEY, CARRIE, THAT TALL, HANDSOME CHARACTER IS DOWN-stairs." Toby stuck his head in the door, smirking. "He asks can he bring up some letters from your homeroom at school?"

"You mean Tom Jenkins?"

"Yeah."

"To see me? No kidding? Hey, Toby, hand me my comb and mirror. Do I look all right? No, I can't see him."

"Don't be so dumb. You look O.K. When you are in bed, nobody can see nothin'. Besides, there's nothin' to see!"

"Oh, shut up."

"Look, I got an idea. Take these pillows and roll them up. They'll look like legs. See?"

"Toby, you're a genius." She threw back the covers.

Toby paled as he saw the elastic-bandaged stumps below her short pajamas. He gently placed the pillows and helped her sit up higher. Then he covered her and straightened the blue spread.

"There. You look great. 'Cept you need some lipstick. Here. I'll go get old Tom."

"You be good."

Soon Toby showed Tom in.

"Hi, Carrie." He came and stood near the bed.

"Hi, Tom."

"The class said since I was president, I should bring you these." He gave her a folder full of letters.

"Thanks. Can you stay? Please sit down." She saw the long red scar on his forehead at the edge of his hair.

"How come you won't let Mrs. Green come see you?"

"You should know."

"The teacher thinks you blame her for what happened. It wasn't her fault. She's a good driver. You know that. She feels bad enough . . ."

"Please. I can't talk about it."

"O.K., Carrie. Has Janey been here? She wants to come so bad. She is still your best friend."

"I haven't seen her yet. I don't want to see anyone who reminds me of what happened. Janey looks like—And I must remind her—And then I have that dream."

"Do you think you are the only one who dreams?"

"Maybe not. But look at me, I can't walk."

"But you don't *look* any different." His fingers unconsciously felt the long red scar on his forehead.

"Oh, yes, I do."

"All the kids will be glad to help you and push your chair. The guys can even carry you upstairs. You'll get along O.K."

"I'll think about it."

"We need some of your terrific posters. The guys aren't doing so well at basketball."

"I can't ever lead yells again."

"We know. But you can yell. And we like you to be there. And you have good ideas for publicity."

"You never noticed."

16

"Oh, yes, we did. You let us know when you can come back. We need you."

"Thanks, Tom. Thank everyone. If you see Janey, tell her to call me, O.K.?"

"Sure. I have to go now. See you."

Carrie hugged herself. He was just the neatest! He hadn't acted funny. Maybe, just maybe, she *would* try that chair. She could just see it all. The big crowd. Her chair pushed into a place of honor by those strong guys on the team.

She took her pencil and paper and sketched. Tom looked a little like that—heavy brows, hair slightly wavy and combed back, straight nose, squinchy eyes, one dimple in left cheek. Hesitantly she added the scar. Then she tucked the drawing under all the blank paper.

She planned out several posters. "Victory for Truman Junior High Sea Gulls."

Mrs. Trent, her visiting teacher, came at ten o'clock for school lessons. It was quite a coincidence that she was Carrie's Sunday school teacher, too. It was much easier than meeting a new person. Besides, she was young and pretty and not a bit square.

They outlined subjects and planned study time. It didn't look as if it would be too hard. Carrie did some studying after Mrs. Trent left.

There was a soft knock at the open door. "Please, can I come in?" It was Sara Riley.

How did she get past Mother and Toby?

"I sneaked in. I had to see you."

"Why?"

"You don't look different. Toby said you were flat where your legs are 'sposed to be. What happened to you?"

17

"Well, I went out in a boat all by myself. Way out in the ocean. Miles from land. A shark began to swim around me. I got scared. I yelled and yelled. The shark bumped the boat. I hit him with the oar. He rammed the boat and I tipped over. He went chomp—one leg gone. He went chomp—two legs gone. I fainted."

"What happened?"

"I don't know. I fainted."

"But—"

"I got rescued by the Coast Guard. Whole bunch of young handsome guys."

"I don't believe you."

"Ask Toby."

"O.K., I will. What are you drawing?"

"Stuff."

"Draw me something."

"O.K. Sit over there and shut up."

Quickly Carrie drew an ugly bratty girl with untidy braids, staring eyes, a long nose, and teeth sticking out. It did look like Sara, except the nose was extra long.

"Here. Now beat it."

"That's not me."

"It is too. You're a nosy brat."

"You're not very nice."

"Neither are you. Now get lost."

"You're mean. And nasty. And you got no legs, and I'm glad."

She ran out as Carrie barely missed hitting her with a book.

Carrie rang the bell. No one came. She sat, twisting her new ring on her finger. When she felt like this, the blue stone had to be turned inside her hand. It was like an eye, telling her to be good.

Once her phone was in, she would be able to call anyone. Now no one answered when she rang. It was so quiet and hot. She threw back the covers. That was no good. There were those cut-off legs. They were hurting, too. Move them, everybody said. You have to move them, so you can get up and not get dizzy. Don't forget your exercises. Do special sit-ups and push-ups. Move your knees. Rub your legs. Your arms have to be especially strong, too.

Oh, yuk!

She turned on the television. Dumb old cartoons. Sickening.

The kids' letters. They all said, "We miss you. Come back soon." They told of all kinds of activities she was missing.

She felt so horrible.

The front door banged shut, and Daddy yelled, "I'm home." Even that sounded so—so childish.

He ran upstairs, hurried into her room, lifted her—covers and all—and put her on the couch.

"It's so great to have you home," he said, kissing her.

"You hurt me."

"Honey, I'm sorry."

"Please put me back."

"A change is good for you," he told her.

"No."

"A surprise?"

"Just put me back. Where is Mother?" Carrie asked.

"O.K., Honey. I'll find her for you." He gently made her comfortable and went out quietly.

Carrie felt meaner than ever. Her ring was still turned in.

Angel in her nurse's outfit grinned at her. Carrie opened the drawer and threw the doll in, catching her finger as she slammed it shut.

"OH—oh—oh—" she screamed. She rang her bell frantically and then threw it out the door into the hall, almost hitting her mother.

"Do I dare come in?" she asked gently. .

"Yes. Please."

"Do you like the way you treated Daddy?"

"Well—"

"Even being tired and in pain is no excuse to hurt people," her mother continued.

"They hurt me."

"You will have to learn to be the strong one who can take it."

"Don't always preach at me!"

"Carrie."

"I mean it. Do this. Don't do that. Be sweet. Be kind. Smile. Yuk!"

Mother turned to leave. "I told you, I won't stay when you are unpleasant."

Carrie was surprised to find that she could be sweet outside and still feel sandpapery inside.

"I'm sorry, Mother."

"You are to apologize to your father."

"Yes, Mother."

The blue stone on her ring still stayed hidden inside her hand.

4

THINGS WERE GOING BETTER. HER PHONE WAS IN AND SHE could call her friends and buzz for Mom downstairs. Janey came often on her way home from school.

Janey Folsom had always been her best friend since they were little kids. She and her family lived in the next block. Everybody said they looked good together because Janey had dark hair and brown eyes. They had been the same height. They had been yell leaders together.

It had been hard for both of them to see each other at first, because Janey and her older sister had been with them that horrible night. It was something they couldn't talk about. Not yet. Maybe someday. Until then, things couldn't be quite right.

Mother usually had a snack ready when Janey came. They gabbed fast, and Carrie began to keep up with all the news. Janey helped her with schoolwork, too. Often she stayed and had dinner on a tray in Carrie's room.

Carrie used the couch or the big chair now. She still refused to try the wheelchair on her own. And when company came, she used the rolled-up pillows where her feet should be.

Tom dropped by again with two other boys. They wanted

her to do some posters for the Spring Festival. She said she would.

She seldom had the dream anymore. She felt much stronger.

Dr. Blain came one afternoon. He poked and pinched and pricked her with a pin. She did what he told her without a word, but she felt herself getting mad.

"Well, young lady, as soon as you wish we will start the next step. Your mother can make an appointment to take you in for a fitting right away. As you know, your new legs were measured and ordered while you were in the hospital. Now you go for fittings and adjustments."

He patted her shoulder and continued, "We will set up regular appointments at the hospital in physiotherapy for about three times a week. You will be an outpatient. That means you don't need to stay all the time. It won't really take long, Carrie. It's not nearly as hard as you think. You will be on your way before you know it."

"I won't."

"Carrie," her mother warned.

"I am not going to stump around on wooden legs, and canes, and crutches."

"We explained right at first that modern—"

"I don't care."

"Mrs. Karns, I thought a little time at home—She is strong and young. The development and shaping of the stumps is excellent."

Carrie was just about to explode. She knew she was red and hot.

"Doctor, perhaps we should discuss this downstairs." Mrs. Karns took him out and shut the door.

Go back for treatment? Never!

Get up and walk? Impossible!

Heavy wooden legs—fake feet? No, thank you!

So they weren't wooden. No filmy nylons and high heels. Braces and belts and metal. It was so horrible to think about.

Oh, sure, everyone said they weren't bad. If you had good balance and coordination, it was simple. They could say it! It wasn't them.

Wonder what Mom and the doctor are saying? She couldn't quite hear. If only the door were open. She heard Daddy drive in. Now there would be a real conference.

The wheelchair had been left within reach. Pull it over by the bed. Lock the wheels. Sit up. Pull yourself over by it. Lift out the near arm of the chair. Hold on to the far arm. Lift yourself over. Pull your legs carefully. Hey, it was easy. Sure she remembered directions. She had paid attention even if she hadn't let them know.

Replace the arm. Unlock the wheels. It was a cinch. She rolled to the door and set the brakes. Very carefully, she opened the door.

Dr. Blain was just leaving. "That's it, Mr. and Mrs. Karns. We have gone as far as we can without her cooperation. She has to do things for herself. We know she is capable. She could be walking within weeks. This block of hers is becoming alarming."

"Yes, sir." Daddy's voice sounded discouraged.

"I will call that psychiatrist, Dr. Wycoff, if you wish."

"Wait another week, please," Mother said in her quiet voice.

"Very well. Good day, folks."

The front door closed. Very quickly Carrie got back into bed. It really seemed quite easy. She almost laughed out loud. Anytime she wanted, she could use that chair.

Dr. Wycoff? Oh, yes. She had met him. But there was

23

nothing wrong with her brain. Just her no feet!

She had heard all the talk. I have to want to get up, she thought. Well, I don't. Not and have all the kids call me Stumpy. And wear dowdy old clothes. Let whoever wanted come to her. She could do things right in her own room.

She didn't take her capsule that night. She wanted to try the chair again. She waited until the house was settled for the night and then reached for her robe. She could dress herself, too. And do the bandages. And everything. But nobody needed to know that. All that talk of A.D.L.—activities of daily living—the nurses raved about and insisted that she learn. It was a laugh. She could do it all if she wanted.

Slowly and quietly she got into her chair. The night-light in the hall was enough to see by. It was very quiet. Little by little she pulled the cord that opened the drapes. It was a beautiful spring night. The streetlight on the corner made a stage for a proud Siamese cat, which performed a graceful dance chasing a moth.

Then a couple strolled by. It was that stuck-up college girl in the next block. The boy was tall and very skinny. At the edge of the light, he pulled her around to kiss her. She slapped him. It sounded so funny.

A car went by. She was getting sleepy. Another car passed, going very slowly. It was dark with a lighter top.

Just as she started to close the drapes, the car passed again. The same one. She waited. Several minutes passed. Then for the third time she saw the same car. It stopped at the corner facing her. Four men got out and opened the trunk. They scarcely made a sound, looking all around.

She leaned forward. The license was shadowed but it looked like B F O or B E D.

A dark panel truck drove up and stopped beside the car.

Quietly some things were carried and placed in the truck. Not big things—one man could carry each. Then they drove off in different directions.

She closed the drapes and got back in bed. What she had seen didn't seem important, except that they had been so careful, looking around and not making noise. She would tell Daddy about it in the morning.

5

"CARRIE, YOUR LESSONS ARE BEAUTIFULLY DONE," MRS. TRENT said. "Wish all my home students did half as well."

"They are easy and I have plenty of time."

"Mrs. Green, your homeroom teacher, is very anxious to see you. She is such a nice person. She has outlined all of your work and has spent a lot of time on it."

"I know. Please thank her for me."

"Won't you let her come see you?"

"No."

"Why not, Carrie? You must have a reason."

"I have."

"Can't you tell me?"

"Every time I even half think of what happened, I have the most awful dream, as if it were happening all over again. I just can't!"

"Maybe seeing her would help. She thinks you blame her. It wasn't her fault."

"No. I know, but—"

"May I tell her she can come?"

"No. I just can't. Please don't ask."

"All right, Carrie. May I ask something else? When will you

come to Sunday school? We really miss you."

"I don't believe it."

"We have all been praying for you. You would be surprised at how many friends you have. You are an unusual girl, Carrie. Your enthusiasm sparks others. You make things interesting and alive."

"Maybe I used to. Not anymore."

"There is no reason to feel you have changed that much. Of course you are different, but in a richer, deeper way. You have faced things that few people ever have to think about. You can benefit by it, if you really try."

"Please, Mrs. Trent, don't you psych me, too. It's easy to say, but I just can't feel that way."

"You can, if you think it through. You have everything going for you. O.K., I'm leaving. I just hate to see a nice person like you give up. I promise I won't talk like this again unless you bring it up first. Forgive me?"

"I guess."

She left. Carrie almost cried. Mrs. Trent was so slim and beautiful. Her legs were pretty and she had on green high-heeled pumps to match her green knit suit. She looked exactly the way Carrie wanted to and now never would.

The light caught in the blue stone of her ring and twinkled at her. She wiped a tear on her flowered robe.

"Hi, Honey. Got a kiss for old Dad?" He came sweeping in and put a big box in her lap.

Inside was a lovely soft flowered sweater in shades of orange, gold, and brown. Tucked under it was a soft wool skirt that matched the orange in the sweater perfectly.

"It is beautiful, Daddy. Thank you."

"I want to take my family out to dinner tonight. Now I

27

won't take no for an answer. Put on your new duds and let's go."

"But, I—"

"Don't say it." Then Dad called to Toby, "Clean up, we're going to the Hilltop for chow."

"But Mother—"

"I called her from the office. Let's go."

Mother came in looking very lovely in a soft yellow wool dress. Her hair was piled high and the reddish lights showed in her brown hair.

Daddy kissed her and went to get ready.

Carrie hadn't been fully dressed for a long time. It felt good. The sweater was so pretty. Her scarf looked just right with it. The skirt fit well, too. Mother had knit some dark-brown stump socks to cover the elastic bandages. When Carrie sat still, the skirt was full enough to cover her stumps completely.

It really was almost too much to face to look below the skirt and see nothing. Save money on shoes anyhow, and nylons. Tears were close again.

The family didn't give her a chance to back out. Daddy carried her to the car and put her gently into the front seat. They all climbed in and were off. Everyone was trying to be so cheerful.

Carrie had to admit it was fun. She noticed that Daddy was driving extra carefully. It was just getting dark and it was beautiful. Lights were coming on. Spring flower smells filled the air. Little kids were still playing outside, laughing and shouting happily.

They went past the school, deserted now but looking the same as ever. On the next corner was the Icey Spot, where all her friends collected. Only a few cars were there, since it was dinnertime.

The church was the same. It would be nice to get back. She did miss everyone.

The glow lasted even when they parked in the lot by the Hilltop Diner. They got the folding wheelchair and Daddy lifted her into it. No one seemed to notice as Toby pushed her in and up to a table near the door. The wheelchair fit under just right.

This was a fun place to come and, as usual, Carrie had trouble deciding what she wanted to eat. It was almost like old times. Everyone forgot—for a while.

Then a fat little boy spoiled it all.

While Daddy paid the check, he left Carrie sitting beside him in her chair.

The little boy stood right in front of her, his eyes as big as boiled eggs. Then he turned to his mother. "Look, Ma." His voice really carried. "That girl's got no legs or feet. What happened, Ma? What happened?"

Carrie could feel herself getting red and hot.

The woman was terribly embarrassed. She pulled the boy away and covered up his mouth. He still stared, his eyes huge above her hand.

Mother grabbed for Toby. He was really winding up a punch for the fat little kid.

Daddy pushed Carrie out the door without waiting for change.

They just sat in the car.

Toby exploded first. "Why didn't you let me flatten that—that—"

"Simmer down, Toby," Daddy ordered. "It is something we have to learn to take calmly."

Carrie saw that the whole family was upset. "I guess so," she

29

heard herself say. "I am different. I always will be. Thanks, Toby. You're a good kid."

"Right, Son," Daddy added. "But hitting just doesn't solve things."

Mother was crying. "We were having such a good time. Carrie looks so pretty. How do you get used to it?"

"You just grow calluses, I guess," Daddy said, starting the motor. "How about a drive-in movie? There is a good one at the Midway."

"Hey, yeah." Toby was all for it.

"How about it, Mother? Carrie?"

They agreed, but the deep hurt wouldn't go completely away.

6

MUCH LATER THAT NIGHT CARRIE WHEELED TO THE WINDOW
and opened the drapes. It had been quite an evening. The
thing she remembered was that the whole family was involved
in her problem. It wasn't just hers alone.

Did she always want to be carried and pushed around? Was
it possible to walk again?

In the dim light from the window she unwrapped her right
leg. The knee looked the same except for a long scar on one
side. Below her knee the leg tapered to a rounded cone shape.
She had heard the doctor's directions that this was how it had
to be and why the elastic bandages had to be kept just so. Then
it would fit into the—the prosthesis (not wooden leg) and
support her so she could learn to walk.

She unwrapped the left one too. It didn't even have a scar.
She felt the bare stumps. It felt good to rub them. They really
didn't hurt. She could rub quite hard. It felt tingly and made
her want to stretch. Something strange—when she rubbed it
right there, she could feel it in her big toe. Except that she had
no big toe!

A car door slammed. She looked out to the street. The same
two-tone car, with the van following, had stopped. Three fel-

31

lows got out, melting into the trees on the school grounds. The car drove away. The van stayed parked in the shadows. Everything was as silent as before.

She heard glass break. She waited, watching and listening. Something was definitely wrong. A light flashed high in the trees. It took her a few seconds to identify the place. It had to be an upper-floor window of the school building. It must be a flashlight. They had broken into the school building.

Better call Daddy? No, the phone. Maybe the police could catch them while they were still there.

She rolled to the phone by her bed and dialed the emergency number. Trying to stay calm, she quickly gave the information. They thanked her politely.

Better call Daddy? He couldn't do anything. It was late. Her little clock said 2:10.

She pushed herself back to the window. The panel truck was still parked across the street. She knew that someone was sitting inside it, because she saw the spurt of fire as a cigarette was lighted.

A man got out, stood listening, and stretched his arms high. He must have been sitting a long time. He was very tall and thin. As he got back in, something dropped. There was no sound, but something glinted as it fell. A spark of light reflected from a metal object. The man didn't notice.

In the distance she heard a siren. Such a sound always made her feel hollow inside, even when she knew it was the police and not an ambulance. It was another of those things not to remember.

The siren was much closer. Quite suddenly someone ran out of the trees, jumped into the panel truck, and it pulled away, fast.

Nothing else happened. She began to notice that she was getting cold. Her legs were still bare. She wrapped them carefully and then got back into bed.

She listened a long time. Then, afraid of dreaming, she reached for the pill Mom had put out for her.

"Carrie. Breakfast."

"Ummm—"

"It's ten o'clock, Sweetie. A beautiful day. Feel like getting dressed? This pair of green shorts would look great with your striped top. Here are your socks. Come on, Honey. Let's move. I want to do the wash. I need your sheets." Mom was rattling. She was nervous.

"What's wrong, Mom?"

"There is a reporter and a photographer from the newspaper downstairs. They want to see you."

"Me?"

"They say you helped catch some vandals breaking in and stealing at the school last night."

"Oh, that."

"I told them it wasn't possible. What could you see from your bed?" She was leaning down and looking out of the window.

"I wasn't in bed."

"You were up? How? Your chair? By yourself? Oh, Carrie."

"Sure, I can work that dumb old chair. It's easy."

"Then you did see something?"

"Yes. I called the police."

"Why, Honey, that's wonderful. I'm so glad!"

"Do I have to see them?"

"Who? Oh, the reporters. I suppose that it won't do any harm. They said they would wait until you are ready."

33

"Not the shorts, Mom. One of my long robes. I'll sit in my chair by the window."

When Daddy carried her upstairs after dinner, he put her on the couch and sat beside her.

"Your picture in the paper looks beautiful. I'm proud of you."

"I didn't see much, Dad."

"What did you see, Carrie? Is the account in the paper correct?"

"Yes."

"They caught two young fellows in the act of stealing expensive equipment: typewriters, mimeographs, tape recorders, cameras, and things like that."

"I read that."

"The point is, Honey, the police think it is a gang that has broken into a number of schools recently. Think over what you saw. If there is anything else you can report, it would help."

"I did see a car and a panel truck. Two different times."

"Was something different about them?"

"Not really. I think I saw some letters on the license plate. It was B F O or B E D. The light was quite dim. I saw the men, but it was much too dark to describe them. One night I saw them change things from the back of the car to the truck. That's about all."

"O.K., Honey. I'll report it. Now, what is this I hear about you getting into your chair by yourself?"

"It's easy."

"You didn't tell anyone! We're so glad you're beginning to do things for yourself."

"Daddy, I don't need any shrink."

"Now, what do you know about that?"

"I talked to that psychiatrist at the hospital. I know what he would say. I just have to work all this out for myself."

"The doctor is concerned, Carrie. The longer you wait to get started learning to walk, the slower and harder it will be. It has to do with your training muscles. You are a strong and active girl."

"I just can't yet."

"There is absolutely nothing to be ashamed of. Lots of people are different."

"I know, but this is me."

"You have so much, Honey, and so many to help you. Even Toby."

"I'll think about it."

"Since you are beginning to try, we are going to go ahead and get the chair elevator installed. It runs on a track right up the stairs."

"I saw one on TV."

"This will help your mother, too. By the way, Carrie, if it's O.K. with you, I'm going to take Mother away for a few days. Have you thought how much you depend on her? She's looking very tired. I think it would do her good."

"Oh, Daddy."

"We will ask Grandma to stay with you and Toby. I know you can manage."

"When, Daddy?"

"I have asked for a week off at the end of the month. We'll go to the ocean. Your mother loves it there."

"But that will be seven whole days."

"Yes. The time will go fast."

"Well—"

"Carrie, I want your cooperation on this. Mother won't go one step if she thinks it will upset you."

"Well—"

"Carrie!"

"O.K., I guess."

"That's my girl. Better hit the books now, Honey. Isn't tomorrow the day for Mrs. Trent?"

7

CARRIE'S DAYS WERE QUITE BUSY: EXERCISES, LESSONS, THANK-you notes and letters, favorite television programs, artwork, and posters.

She had finally let them talk her into visiting the place that was making her substitute legs. They were polite and considerate. She wasn't embarrassed at all. They showed her how the legs would look at first with metal adjustments showing at the ankles. After these were set, they would be covered and the leg and ankle would be smooth. She could wear panty hose and even have another pair of legs later so she could wear high heels.

They suggested that she take them home and look them over and wear them a little. She shoved the box deep into the back of her closet.

She had also consented to help Janey train the yell leaders. They came to the Karns house to practice. At first it had hurt too much to see them dancing and jumping so gracefully. But Carrie found she was a good director, and they really improved. She even thought up some new routines, and everyone liked them very much, the girls said.

She was almost at the point where she was thinking of going to a game.

It was time for her teacher. Carrie was seldom in her bed now. She rolled her chair over and adjusted the drapes and straightened her desk.

"Hi, Carrie." Mrs. Trent greeted her, looking beautiful in a pink wool suit. "I brought two visitors."

Mrs. Green, her homeroom teacher from school, came in. She was limping, her right ankle wrapped. She looked thin and pale. She carried a large box.

"Carrie, I've been so anxious to see you. Please don't throw me out."

"Hello, Mrs. Green."

"Carrie, you look lovely. You know how I've wanted to come see you."

"Yes. It just reminds me—"

"I know. I have nightmares, too."

"You do?"

"Oh, yes. I'm trying to forget, too. And I feel responsible."

There was a scratching sound from the box she held.

"I brought you something. I have your parents' permission. Here."

She placed the box on the desk. Carrie lifted the lid. A tiny white poodle was looking up at her. He had a blue ribbon around his neck, bright-blue eyes, and a red tongue just barely sticking out. He looked as if he was smiling.

"Oh!" She carefully lifted him. He cuddled under her chin.

"He's a miniature. He's already housebroken, so he can stay with you. I have friends who raise them." Mrs. Green's eyes were anxious. "Maybe he will help you forget. Or at least make it easier to face what can't be changed."

Carrie rubbed her tears away in the tiny dog's curly fur.

"Thank you, Mrs. Green. I'm sorry I wouldn't see you."

"Sometimes it is hard to let people share your problems. You are most welcome. The dog has no name. I'm sure he will learn to respond quickly."

Mrs. Trent handed Carrie a package. She opened it. It was a blue-suede harness and leash studded with brilliants. It just fit. Mrs. Green put the little dog on the floor, and he strutted around, proud of himself and getting acquainted.

When Carrie looked up, Toby and Sara were standing in the door. The puppy ran over to them, wiggling all over, almost shaking off his little tufted tail.

"I think it might be a good idea to have the children take him out a few minutes," Mrs. Green said. "This has been quite exciting for him."

"You be careful, Toby. Don't you dare let him get away," Carrie ordered. They fastened his leash on the harness, and he ran ahead of them, anxious to explore.

Pleasantly, the three went over Carrie's schoolwork and planned out the next several weeks.

Mother joined them and exclaimed about the puppy. Only too soon the teachers had to leave.

Carrie hugged Mrs. Green. It surprised them both. "I'll never be able to thank you enough."

"Oh, yes, Carrie. Just walk into my classroom by yourself someday—soon."

Carrie was glad to be alone for a few minutes. She had to cry. It made her mad to do it so often and easily. Mother had said that so much medicine often made a person feel that way. It still was embarrassing.

Toby and Sara came bursting in. The little dog ran ahead of them and leaped up into Carrie's lap, then down. He ran around the room and back to her lap, collapsing, with his tiny red tongue hanging out. She patted his soft woolly fur.

"Can I play with him sometimes?" Toby asked.

"Sure. Somebody will have to take him out now and then. I'll need some help."

"Me too," Sara said. "Just wave out the window and I'll come."

Mother came in and took the dog in her arms. "He's so cute. You're very lucky, Carrie. This kind of dog is very expensive. And to be already trained, too!"

"I know. Just don't anybody forget he's mine."

"Let's call him Lassie," Sara said.

"You are so dumb!" Toby said. "Lassie is a girl's name. Bet that's the only dog name you know."

"Is not."

"Besides, it's up to Carrie to name him. Can I help teach him stuff?"

"Sure, Toby."

"Now run on, youngsters," Mother said. "Time for lunch."

Daddy came up right after he got home from work. "So that's the ferocious animal?" he laughed as the little dog rolled over to have his tummy scratched. "They sure didn't have many scraps left when they made him!"

"Scraps! That's it. That's his name. Scraps! Thanks, Daddy."

"Not a bad name. I'm glad you have him, Honey. By the way, our plans are set for our vacation. The elevator on the stairs will be in, but use Toby for errands as much as you can. Your grandmother isn't too strong."

"I'll miss you."

"I know. But I think it's important. Especially for your mother."

"I guess."

"Carrie, there is something else. The police called me at work. They picked up the car and driver used in the robbery. There were several thousand dollars' worth of stolen property in the trunk. They wanted me to thank you."

"I didn't do much."

"There is a small item in the paper. This worries them because they haven't caught the rest of the gang. They are sure there must be a leader who sells the stuff. If you remember or see—"

"Hi, Dad." Toby came bursting in. "Neat dog, huh?"

"Daddy just named him. He's Scraps."

"I like that. Hi, Scraps." Toby got down on the floor and played with him. Scraps was fast, darting out to attack, jumping back, rolling over. It was so funny watching them. He was so little and so full of energy. Carrie hadn't laughed that hard for a long time.

Scraps kept her awake that night. They had made a comfortable bed in a box with an old sweater. It just fit under the bedside table. But Scraps didn't like it. It was much cozier in bed with Carrie.

Mother had made it quite clear that the puppy should stay in his own bed. Scraps just wouldn't get the message. His tiny little whine and his many wet kisses won Carrie completely. He finally settled down and went to sleep cuddled against her back. At least he wasn't *in* her bed!

As she lay awake, there was something she was trying to remember. Something she hadn't told Daddy about what she had seen.

The phone by her bed rang. She picked it up immediately so it wouldn't wake anyone.

"Hello."

She heard breathing.

"Hello?"

A faint voice said, "Better go to sleep, little girl. Don't pay to look out windows." There was a click and the line was closed.

She felt very cold. Had she reported all of what she had seen? Maybe not. Something about that call frightened her. She had to try to remember.

There certainly was no danger in her own warm bed in her own house. Must just be someone playing tricks.

8

"READY, YOUNG LADY?"

"Not quite, Daddy. Ten minutes more."

Her hair was such an awkward length. She had managed to make it turn under slightly, making it look longer. She brushed it again.

She felt cold and then hot. All day it had been that way. One minute she looked forward to it. The next she was scared to death. But she had promised Janey and Tom.

It was the last game and it was against Garfield, their greatest rival.

Janey had brought the whole yell team and song leaders over in the afternoon and Carrie had gone out on the side porch to advise them as they practiced in the side yard. They had worked out some really good routines.

Carrie had also helped with the advertising and designed a special program with a cartoon cover.

She had finally decided to wear the orange skirt with the flowered sweater Daddy had given her. Mom had bought her a new shade of lipstick that was just right. She dabbed on a touch of flower fragrance.

"Carrie? We will be late."

"O.K., Daddy." She looked at herself again. She had on the brown knit socks and had a soft brown shawl to put over her lap.

She rolled her chair to the top of the stairs. The safety gate was easy to work. She now could lift herself onto the chair elevator. It was fun to push the button and go gliding down. At the bottom another wheelchair was kept that could be used outside. She could even get into that by herself now.

Scraps always enjoyed it when she moved around the house. He ran in circles and yapped in his tiny voice. Just today Daddy had completed the ramp out the back door to the driveway. Mother walked happily beside her as she tried it for the first time.

If she could just stand, even on one leg, she could get in the car by herself.

Daddy drove to the loading zone in front of the gym. Then he got the folding chair from the trunk and lifted her into it.

Almost everyone was inside. In fact, she heard the first notes of "The Star-spangled Banner" being played. A man helped Daddy carry her chair up the few steps.

In the excitement following the national anthem, Daddy wheeled her into place beside the bleachers near the door, the shawl over her knees. A place had been reserved for them.

It was all so exciting. The noise, the color, the smells were all so familiar. She loved it. The kids were beginning to notice. Many were waving. They were introducing the teams. She clapped loudly.

The first yell was great, especially with that cartwheel ending Carrie had suggested. The whistle blew. The game began.

She was completely absorbed—cheering, clapping, shouting.

Daddy put his hand on her arm. "Honey, calm down. You'll fall."

44

She had forgotten. For several whole minutes! It felt so good. She wanted to hug everyone.

She sat back for a second or two, and then was yelling again. Who can be quiet at a basketball game? She scarcely noticed when the shawl fell on the floor, and Daddy folded it and put it beside him on the bench.

At the half Carrie sank back. The team was ahead by six points. Still a close game.

"Tired, Honey?" Daddy asked.

"Oh, no. Thanks for bringing me. It's so great. I've missed it."

Mr. Dean, the principal, was at the loudspeaker. "I have been asked to make a special presentation at this time. We have someone with us tonight we have all been missing. Yet in her enforced absence she has still shown exceptional school spirit. The team and yell staff have asked me to give a special inspirational award to this person. This also comes from the faculty and students. Miss Carrie Karns."

Janey and Tom came over to get her.

"Hi, Carrie! It's great to see you here," Tom said with a big grin.

"You look absolutely wonderful!" Janey beamed.

Together they pushed her chair to the center of the floor. The student body president presented her with a bouquet of red roses, and Mr. Dean gave her a shield-shaped plaque engraved with her name.

"Thank you, oh, thank you."

"Fifteen cheers for Carrie," Janey called. The rafters rang.

Carrie hid her tears in the roses.

The kids swarmed around. The referees whistled furiously to clear the floor. When they wheeled her back, Mom and Toby were there, grinning broadly.

"Some surprise, huh?" Toby yelled.

Mother handed her a hanky. Then Carrie noticed there was no shawl on her knees. It hadn't made a bit of difference.

Her dad had to lift Carrie out of the wheelchair and onto the bench beside him. He was afraid she would fall, the way she was jumping around and yelling. Mom sat on the other side, and Carrie didn't mind when Mom held on to her arm. It was all so exciting!

Everyone was really amused when Carrie got mad and yelled "Down in front" at a quiet moment. People just wouldn't stay out of her way.

It was hard to remember the details afterward. The boys played so smoothly. They scarcely missed a basket. It was unbelievable. Poor Garfield. Final score was 68 to 45! Tom was high scorer with 22 points.

Dad insisted on stopping at the Icey Spot for milkshakes after the game. The car was surrounded by excited, friendly, wonderful kids and teachers.

When Mom tucked her in bed much later, Carrie knew she was very tired, but it felt so good.

"I've never had such a great time! Mom, I actually forgot for a whole long time!"

"I'm glad it went so well. Things can be good again. I'm sure of it, Carrie. Since tomorrow is Sunday, it will be quiet around here. You sleep as long as you can. We will go to church as usual. But one of us will stay here."

"You all go. I can get around."

"Your breakfast?"

"I can get it."

"I know you can, but I worry about those steps when no one is here. If you happened to fall—"

"O.K., Mom." She was too tired to argue.

"I'll leave a tray."

Mother turned off the lamps and said good night. Toby brought Scraps in, but she was too tired to talk.

Scraps curled up in his box. He really was a little stinker. About three seconds after Mom was gone, he was curled up in his favorite spot on the bed by Carrie's back. He seemed to know it saved a scolding to do it that way.

Carrie didn't hear the phone ring.

9

Slowly Carrie awoke. She stretched. It bothered Scraps. He gave a tiny bark and then began to stretch, too. She reached out to pat him and the light caught the blue stone in her ring. She turned it and the reflection winked at her.

She smelled roses. She rolled over, cuddling back into the warmth of her bed, remembering all the things that had happened the night before. She had never had red roses of her own. They looked so beautiful in Mother's best cut-glass vase. Like deep-red velvet. And the perfume, heavenly! Too bad they couldn't stay that way always.

Nothing ever stayed that way always.

Scraps was fussing. He needed to go out. It was so quiet that she felt no one was home. She reached for her robe and swung herself into her chair.

She opened the drapes and could see Sara playing hopscotch on the sidewalk in front of her house. She came running when Carrie waved. In a moment she was in Carrie's room.

"Hi. I said I would watch for you."

"Thanks, Sara. Scraps' leash is by the door."

"I'll be careful. Your mom said I was to bring you some juice and toast, if you want."

48

"O.K., when you come back."

Carrie could manage in the bathroom by herself now. Daddy had put in some handles and a bar. Sure would help if she just had one leg to balance on.

She zipped herself into her long soft-blue robe and went back to the window. Scraps was loose. He ran in speedy circles around and around Sara. She would almost reach the leash and then he would give a little jump. It really looked funny. When Carrie laughed out loud, he heard her and sat to look up at her, his tongue lolling in a silly grin. Sara caught him and carried him, wiggling, into the house.

Scraps came tearing into Carrie's room, grabbed his rubber bone, and leaped into her lap. He left the bone and vaulted down, dancing expectantly, begging her to throw it. She played with him several minutes before Sara came in with a tray.

"How come you're not at church?" Carrie asked.

"Momma said I didn't have to go. We're having company. I'm helping her."

"You are? Some helper!" Carrie laughed.

"I said I'd help you, too."

"Oh. I'm sorry."

"Why don't you like me, Carrie?"

"I do."

"No, you don't. You draw bad pictures of me. You tell me stories. Tell me how you lost your legs, Carrie. No one will talk about it."

"Well, you see, it was a dark, stormy, icy night. I was going to the library. I slipped and slid right under a—bulldozer. It rolled over my legs and squashed them."

"That's not true."

"How do you know?"

" 'Cause bulldozers don't work on cold, icy nights. And

49

besides, your mom wouldn't let you go out. I know, you were in an accident and somebody got killed."

"You shut up!"

"It's true. It's true!"

"That's why I don't like you, Sara. You're nosy and you talk too much."

"I brought you toast. I took care of Scraps."

"You are good at times."

"I'm sorry I bugged you." Sara picked up Scraps and held him.

"O.K. Forget it. Only don't you ever ask me again—about that—"

"I won't. Draw me a good picture. Please?"

"What of?"

"Draw a funny picture of Scraps."

"He won't sit still long enough. But I'll try."

She wheeled over to the desk. As she reached for her sketching pencil, the light glinted on the blue stone in her ring. She looked at it. It reminded her of something. A tall thin man stretching. Light glinting.

"Hey, Sara, I just thought of something. Come over here by the window. Look there by the curb, in front of those bushes," she pointed.

"I don't see anything."

"Go over there and look in the dirt and leaves by the curb. Scuff around about as wide as a parked car. There should be a shiny piece of metal."

"How do you know?"

"I don't for sure. How about looking? If you don't want to, I'll ask Toby when he comes home."

"No. I'll do it. You will draw a picture of Scraps for me?"

"I will. Not a bad one either."

50

"Can I take Scraps?"

"O.K. Only don't let go of the leash out on the street."

Carrie watched as Sara came out the front door. She had trouble keeping from getting tangled in Scraps' leash. He was really trying to get loose. They crossed the street, and Carrie waved directions to Sara.

Sara scuffed her feet back and forth. She didn't seem to mind getting her shoes dirty—the street sweeper hadn't been by for quite a while.

Something jingled. Sara bent down and picked up an object that glinted. She held it up, checked the street for cars, and then ran all the way up to Carrie's room, Scraps scampering behind.

"I found it. It looks like a bracelet. Look."

"Sara!" a voice called.

"Oh, that's my mom. I'd better go. I'll come back later." Sara waved and hurried out.

Carrie wiped the bracelet off with a tissue. It was a man's identification bracelet, like the one her dad had worn when he was in the Navy.

"Carrie." Mom called from downstairs. The family was home. She wrapped the object quickly and shoved it in her pocket.

It was late that night before Carrie thought of what she had found. She got out of bed and into her chair and wheeled to the closet. She found it in her robe pocket.

For some reason she didn't turn on her light. There was a small flashlight in her desk drawer. She used it.

There was a name, and numbers, on a smooth metal plate, and then a chain dangling. One link had broken.

"Wight, Daniel Roman O–8632–021." There were other

letters, well worn and not clear. It looked very similar to Daddy's.

She rolled to the window. She was very startled to see a panel truck parked in front. A tall thin man was bent over looking along the curbing.

She drew back and then leaned forward, watching.

He was scuffing his feet. Suddenly he looked up. He saw her. She knew he did. The streetlight!

He hurried to the truck, got in, and drove quickly out of sight. She had no chance to see the license plate.

She rewrapped the bracelet and put it in the drawer by her bed. Slowly she got back under the covers. She must tell Daddy first thing tomorrow. Something was very wrong. That had looked like the same man she had seen on the night of the robbery. He must be part of the gang. The truck looked the same, too.

The phone rang. It really startled her. She picked it up.

"I think you have something of mine. You put it back where you found it—and forget the whole thing—or I'll get that little dog of yours. Don't forget, kid."

The connection went dead. Better call the police. Would they believe her? She did have the bracelet to show. Yet it wasn't possible for the police to watch over a small dog or her family all the time. Was it?

She could have Sara put the chain back. Would that satisfy him? That should solve the whole thing and not cause any more trouble.

It was too much to decide. Nothing must happen to Scraps, though. She rubbed his soft, fuzzy ear.

She would have Sara put the bracelet back first thing tomorrow.

10

WHY WAS IT DOCTORS ALWAYS MADE HER SO MAD? CARRIE definitely felt hot and red. Dumb old doctor! He had said she must start organized treatment at once or it would be too late.

She had improved! She could do almost anything for herself. Maybe she just didn't want to walk, ever. It was too much! Dozens of trips for therapy and fittings. All that pain and bother. They said it wouldn't be so bad now. They said . . . they said . . .

Mrs. Trent arrived soon after the doctor left. She had on her green high heels again and a pretty flowered cotton sleeveless dress.

"Hi, Carrie. Work all done as usual?"

"Yes."

"Wish all my students were like you."

"No, you don't."

"I didn't mean—This is not a good day, I see."

"Have to start regular treatments. Every other day."

"For your training? Good. I'll work out a schedule so there will be no problem. I hear they don't expect it to be very long for you."

"They—they always have big ideas."

53

"Carrie, you are young and strong."

"I still can hurt. And be tired. And ache."

"We all can at times, in different ways. You have to decide what you yourself really want. Do you want to be someone who always has to be helped? Someone who never can be completely alone? Who must always and forever be dependent on others?"

"I don't know."

"Did you see the feature article in the Sunday paper, the magazine section? That man was walking and he had lost two legs and an arm, too. Did you see the look on his face? He has plans to be a teacher. I'll bet he makes it."

"He's a man."

"Smarter? Men are better?"

"Well, no. He's stronger."

"I doubt that. He doesn't have your youth, or your muscular coordination, and probably not your talent or brains."

"I can't be a physical education teacher."

"That is probably true."

"I could teach—"

"Art, design, or just little kids. There are all kinds of possibilities. You are a warm, understanding person. Much more than those who haven't had your sad experience."

"I've got to think about it."

"Time is running out, Carrie."

Sara burst into the room without knocking. "A man took Scraps—"

"What?"

She was panting. "I was in the side yard. Scraps was playing chase. I noticed a man watching. Suddenly he grabbed Scraps. He ran."

"Where? When?"

"Just now!"

"Call the police. Get Daddy."

"Wait, Carrie." Mrs. Trent was at the window. "Scraps is tied to the light post at the corner."

Sara ran. Carrie went to the window. Scraps was there. Tied to the post. Barking madly and furiously. They watched Sara pick him up and try to soothe him.

In a few minutes she gave the still angry puppy to Carrie. He was trying so hard to tell what had happened to him that they had to laugh.

"What a strange thing to happen," Mrs. Trent commented. "Why should anyone do such a thing?"

"Maybe Scraps bit him and he had to put him down," Sara suggested.

"I doubt if Scraps would tie himself to the post."

"Oh, yeah, I forgot."

"At least we have him back," Mrs. Trent said. "I suggest we skip lessons today, Carrie. I will leave these assignments for you to work on. I'll see you day after tomorrow. Better tell your dad what happened." She left quietly.

"I'm awful sorry," Sara said. "Something always goes wrong when I take Scraps out."

"It's not your fault, Sara. Let me think." She went to the drawer by her bed. Then at her desk she made a copy of the information on the identification tag.

"Here, Sara. Put this back in as near the same place as you got it. Please do it right now."

"This has something to do with the dog?"

"It might. Will you please?"

"O.K. Can I come back?"

"Sure. The drawing of Scraps is almost done for you."

"Are you going to tell your dad?"

"I don't know. Maybe nothing else will happen."

"But the man could hurt Scraps."

"He didn't though. Please take this. If you see him again, be sure to tell me."

Toby came in to watch television that evening as he often did. He sat on the floor and played with Scraps. At break time Carrie asked, "Hey, Toby, did Sara tell you what happened this afternoon?"

"Huh-uh."

"A man ran away with Scraps."

"What?"

She told him everything that had happened about the dog.

"Where is he? I'll break his neck."

"Take it easy," Carrie said. "There was no harm done."

"Yeah, but maybe he'll do it again."

"I don't think so. I have his name. I copied it. I'll have Daddy give it to the police."

"Wonder if he could be the man I saw?" Toby questioned.

"When? Where?"

"Some tall guy was picking something up across the street when I was coming back from the store," Toby told her.

"Where?"

"By the curb. He was tall and skinny."

"Could be. Did he say anything?" asked Carrie.

"No. But he sure glared at me."

"Did you see what he picked up?"

"Huh-uh."

"I wonder—"

"Be quiet now, Carrie. I want to watch the rest of this show."

Carrie had lost interest. She went to the desk to get the

paper. She had better give it to Daddy tonight. She had such a way of forgetting things.

Under the blotter. It wasn't there. In the top drawer. No. Now think. She had been at the desk when she wrote it. It was when Sara was going to return the bracelet. They had been very excited.

Where could it be? She hunted methodically through her desk. It was not there.

Mother and Daddy came in to announce bedtime. For some reason she didn't want to bother Dad until she found the paper. It was so stupid to misplace it. She signaled to Toby not to say anything. She should have told the police instead of putting the bracelet back. But all she could think of was Scraps.

Tomorrow she would hunt thoroughly. It had to be here somewhere!

11

EVERYTHING SEEMED TO BE GOING SO MUCH BETTER UNTIL Carrie had the dream again. It was so horrible, real, and painful that she woke screaming and fighting. Mom and Dad and Toby came running. Mom cuddled her and Dad held her hand. Toby had to hold Scraps because he was barking and whining.

"It's O.K., Honey. It's over and you're home and safe," Daddy told her.

"I thought I had forgotten and wouldn't ever dream that again," Carrie said, wiping her eyes on her pajama sleeve. "It was so awful!"

"Your nerves are not completely healed yet," Mom said calmly. "Also, sometimes strong medicine reacts."

They waited silently a moment or two. Daddy stood up to leave. "Come on, Toby. Put Scraps in his box. Let's go back to bed."

"Daddy, please stay. I'm afraid. If I go to sleep again—I'll dream. It will all happen again."

"Really, Honey, I don't think so. Now that you're awake and know where you are—"

"Mom?"

"I'll stay for a while. Daddy, say a prayer for us before you go."

Carrie didn't shut her eyes. She looked at her little brother holding the fuzzy little dog. Then at her dad standing with his head bowed and saying those soothing words. Mom sat close with her arms around her. The lamp made a circle of light and warmth.

She didn't wake up until almost noon. Her head ached and she felt heavy and ugly. It was no use trying to do anything.

She refused to get up, and Mom humored her. She just stayed propped up on pillows, staring out of the window, trying not to think about anything.

Then she heard Mom bringing someone up the stairs to see her. She wanted to object, but it took too much effort.

"Hello, Carrie. Been quite a few days since I've seen you."

It was Pastor Marsh. Usually he was one of her favorite visitors. He was young and good-looking, with friendly eyes and a happy smile. He was so enthusiastic and excited about everything. He always had funny stories to tell.

Mom made an excuse and left them together.

Scraps recognized a friend and presented his bone for a game of chase. Pastor Marsh sat in the big chair and laughed heartily at Scraps' silly antics.

Carrie just watched.

"Your mother said you had a bad night. I'm sorry, Carrie."

"It's O.K."

"Not really, is it?" He held Scraps to quiet him, and the little dog relaxed on his lap.

"Everything was beginning to go so well," Carrie answered.

"That's apt to happen," he said, scratching Scraps' tiny ears.

"Just reminds me. It's no use to even try. Nothing will change."

"You won't get your feet back."

"Exactly," Carrie agreed.

"Lots of people live without feet, or hands, or eyes—"

"That's easy for you to say."

"I know, Carrie. No one can understand exactly how you feel. That's impossible."

"And don't you preach at me."

"It would be easy, but you know all those words, I'm sure."

"Yeah, everybody tells me."

"O.K., Carrie. Do you love your little brother?"

"Toby? Sure."

"Your mother said he didn't want to go to school this morning. He was worried about you."

"I don't believe it."

"It's true. Your dad was worried, too. He called and asked me to come see you."

"So I have him to thank."

"Did you look at your mother this morning? There are dark circles under her eyes, and she keeps rubbing her forehead."

"So—"

"Carrie, it is not just you that is involved in all of this. Now wait"—he held up his hand—"every one of us is affected."

"I'll go away. By myself."

"You know better than that. Or do you want to live the next sixty years or so in a nursing home?" Mr. Marsh asked.

"Sixty years?"

"You have the rest of your life."

"How awful—"

"That's right. How do you want to spend it, Carrie?"

"Go away!"

"O.K., Carrie." He stood up, putting Scraps beside her on the bed. "We really care. Expect to see you in church soon. Bye now."

She felt very alone. Many times she had tried to pray. Somehow, God had deserted her. She threw back the covers and held up her legs. Two stumps! How could He let this happen to her?

She turned over and cried, muffling her sobs in her pillow.

Scraps tried to find her face, growling and tugging. She put one arm around him and hugged him against her face. He licked her tears.

Mom came in and went straight to her closet. "Sorry to bother you, Sweetie, but we have to get ready for your doctor's appointment."

Carrie made her body cooperate. She still hurt inside. There seemed to be no solution.

They had worked out a system for getting into Mother's car. Carrie could do it alone, with Mother to steady her.

Carrie put up with the fittings for her legs and feet. She did just what they told her to do. She stood. She took a step or two. But they had to really hold on, and the crutches were a vital necessity. She wouldn't try anything on her own. She wouldn't even strap on the legs and feet for herself. She just couldn't. Not even when Mother came right out and asked.

Carrie knew Daddy really wanted to scold her when he came home. He just looked at Carrie, gave her a kiss, started to say something, and then left her room.

Later Mom came up with TV dinners on trays for Carrie and Toby. "Daddy insists that he take me out to dinner. I hope you don't mind?"

"Of course not, Mother," Carrie said. "I'm sorry I'm so stupid!" She was twisting the ring on her finger.

"You could make things much easier for everyone, if you wished. Especially for yourself." Mother kissed her and left hurriedly. She looked as if she was about to cry. Carrie felt terrible.

Toby and Scraps came bursting in. "Let's eat. I'm starved." He flipped on the television, set up a folding tray, and began to eat.

Scraps had eaten. He went to sleep on a soft pillow in the big chair.

Carrie picked at her food. It tasted all right but she wasn't hungry. Dad and Mom were both disgusted with her. In fact, she was disgusted with herself.

The fake legs were really pretty neat. They hadn't hurt nearly as much as she had expected. Why did she act so dumb?

Mother knew she felt bad after the fitting and offered to help her pick out a new bathing suit. The doctor had said swimming would be good for her.

Swimming? Bare stumps? No way!

She threw a spoon clear across the room. It scared Scraps. He woke up and started to bark.

"Aw, Sis! Cut it out," Toby complained.

"Turn that TV off," Carrie yelled. "Get out of here."

"O.K., O.K. I'll be in my room if you want me." Even Toby seemed to understand when she felt bad. He didn't act mad at all. Scraps yapped at her and went with Toby.

Everything was wrong. Everyone was mad at her. She couldn't find that scrap of paper. She began going through the drawers of her desk again, throwing stuff on top. A big pile collected. Still no note.

Scraps came running in. He jumped into the big chair, then to its back, and onto the desk. He skidded in the pile of papers, scattering them in all directions. He was trying to lick her face.

It was obvious that he was sorry he had barked at her. He sat in the middle of the papers—tiny tail spreading more destruction—begging to be forgiven.

Carrie lifted him up and cuddled him. Papers were still drifting to the floor. Now poor tired Mother would have more to clean up. She couldn't ask Toby after having been so mean to him.

Maybe she could do it herself. Bet she could! She wheeled to the bed and lifted herself onto it. Lucky she had on shorts! She rolled over on her stomach and pushed herself off the bed. She was kneeling and it didn't hurt! Her knees were O.K. She backed up. She could crawl! It was easy!

She crawled over by her desk, cleared a place, and sat on the floor. By moving only a little, she easily picked up all the papers and, reaching up, put them on top of the desk.

Then she knew what had happened to that note. This same thing had happened before. Scraps had knocked over a pile of papers. Mom had asked if they were important. Carrie had said no, so they were thrown out. She had thought they were just old sketches.

So, the note was gone. That left no proof of any kind to show about the man who had taken Scraps. If only she could remember. Nothing! Maybe she would remember later.

It was fun to sit on the floor. It gave a very different view of things. Her closet door was open. The box with her legs was sticking out. She crawled over to push it out of sight. Instead, she opened it. She could put them on herself. It was easy. They fit well.

They were smooth and shapely and flesh-colored. She had thought they would move at the ankle, but they didn't. Parts of the feet were heavy rubber, so you rocked forward on them as you took a step. Right now there were adjustment screws and bolts at the ankle. Later these would be covered by the same material as the rest of the legs. The straps above the knees came from inside and were padded and they buckled easily. They would be easier to put on if she were sitting on the bed or in her chair. They didn't look too bad.

Toby peeked around the corner and hurried in. "Hey, are you O.K.? Did you fall? Are you hurt? Hey, those look neat. Can you work them?"

"Sure. Nothing to it."

"Let's see."

"I'm just supposed to wear them and get used to them."

"Why don't you? They sure look better than nothing."

"Guess you're right," Carrie agreed.

"Can I help you up?"

"No, I'll do it myself."

She unstrapped the legs and crawled to the bed. Then she rose on her knees, and by putting one knee up, got onto the bed. Then she sat up and lifted herself back into her chair.

"That's great," Toby said. "You really can get around."

Carrie rubbed her knees. They were rather tender. She would have to practice more.

"Here. Now put these on again," Toby said, as he handed her the legs.

It was easier than on the floor. The soft stump socks were kept in the cone-shaped top of the legs. She put them on and then slipped her stumps down into the padded tops. She fastened the straps above her knees.

Toby turned down the little metal steps of the chair and she rested her feet on them. The legs really didn't look bad at all. They felt a little heavy, but they didn't hurt anyplace. They were comfortable.

"I know where your shoes are," Toby said. "Socks, too. Mom kept them. They are in a box in the attic."

In a few minutes he was back with green socks and a pair of low shoes. He put them on for her. The socks covered the adjustment screws and bolts in the ankle area and the shoes fit perfectly. The legs were heavy when she held her feet out to admire them. It would take a little while to get used to them, but they didn't hurt. In fact, they felt and looked good.

Carrie and Toby heard the car drive in. "Let's surprise Mom and Dad," Toby suggested.

Carrie nodded.

It was wonderful to see how their faces lighted up when they saw her sitting there with shoes, socks, and legs.

Daddy pushed her chair around and around in circles, laughing. Scraps barked and barked. Mom just beamed!

12

Mrs. Riley finally left. Her visits really bothered Carrie but her mother insisted that she always be courteous. Mrs. Riley just talked and talked about her ailments, her relatives, her church, and on, and on.

Carrie half listened, sketching various things on her art pad. She had to put her hand over the ugly witch that insisted on coming out of the paper.

Sara asked to stay. "Did you find the paper with that man's name?"

"I guess it's gone."

"How come?"

"Scraps knocked it off the desk to the floor. Mom threw it away when she cleaned up. She didn't know and I forgot."

"Maybe it's all over. That man got his bracelet."

"How do you know?" Carrie asked.

"Toby saw him."

"How come Toby told you?"

"He yelled at me because I let the dog get away. Honest, Carrie, I didn't mean to."

"I'm not blaming you."

"Hey, Carrie, I have an idea. Why don't you draw that man's picture?"

"I didn't see him plain enough."

"Toby and I saw him. We could tell you."

"Let's try."

"I gotta go now but I'll come back after dinner."

When Sara finally came, Toby reluctantly turned off the television. He didn't really want to miss his favorite program but he didn't complain too much.

They gathered around the desk. Carrie adjusted the light. She had drawing paper and pencils handy.

"Make the face like this." Sara outlined a shape with her hands.

Carrie sketched a long thin face, full view. "How about hair?" she asked.

"I think he was getting bald," Sara said.

"Yeah. His forehead was real high and the rest of his hair was all messed up and kinda long," Toby added.

"He had big eyebrows—"

"And bones in his face like an Indian. He glared at me and his eyes were—beady," Toby added.

"That looks like him," Sara said excitedly.

"What did his mouth look like?"

"I don't remember."

Toby frowned. "Thin lips."

"Like this?"

"No." Toby made his own lips in almost a straight line. "More like this."

"That's it," Sara said.

"Something's wrong. He doesn't look right," Toby objected.

"He doesn't have ears yet, stupid," Sara said. "They were flat. Funny and flat."

"Hey, Sis, that's neat!"

"Real good, Carrie," Sara added.

"O.K. Toby, go get Daddy."

"Now? You're going to tell him?"

"Yes. Now. The paper tonight reported another school broken into. Those men are still working. We better stop them if we can."

Toby went to the door and called to Dad, who answered and came right upstairs.

"What's up, kids?" He came in and sat in the big chair. Scraps jumped into his lap.

"Let me tell," Toby demanded.

Finally, with help from all three, the story was told.

"This the man? A very good drawing, Carrie."

"It looks a lot like him," Sara said.

"I wish you had told me before, Carrie. This is serious."

"I'm sorry, Dad. I'm ashamed when I forget things."

"You still can't remember the name?"

"No. The bracelet was the same shape as yours, though."

"That could mean he might have been in the Navy at one time. That, with his picture, just may be enough."

"I hope so," Carrie said.

"I'm going to go down to the Police Department now. I want to caution you three. Don't say one word to anyone. Stay with people and stay in the yard. Don't forget for one minute."

"Would he really do something to us?" Sara asked, her eyes big and staring.

"He might, I'm afraid. If he would take a dog to scare you—"

"Hey, Dad, can I go with you?"

68

"No, Toby. Please don't tell your mother. Now, no more—no more discussion at all. Leave it all to me."

As the days went by, the bracelet was all but forgotten.

One afternoon Carrie stretched out flat on her bed. Wow, she was tired! It was good to be home and alone for a few minutes. She had changed from a skirt and sweater to her at-home clothes. Most comfortable were colorful shirts and shorts. She had several outfits and even stump socks to match.

She could really get around now, all over her room, crawling, kneeling, and using her chair. She also did most things for herself.

Today had really been rough. The workout at the hospital had been extra tiring. She knew it was her own fault. She just couldn't make herself try. She did what they asked her, and that was all.

Why did she feel so stubborn? It did feel good to stand. She was quite sure she could get the balance of walking if she wanted to.

Janey and the girls had just left. Together they had made favors for the Award Banquet for Friday night. They had made pipestem cleaner basketball players and yell leaders, flags, a miniature band, and other decorations.

Carrie would finish the huge picture of the school tower to be placed behind the speaker's table. It was laid out on the floor of the family room downstairs. That had been easy. She was good at crawling and it was fun to paint such a big thing.

The phone rang. "Hello."

"Hi, Carrie." It was Tom Jenkins.

"Hi, Tom."

"I'm sorta late, but—could I—would you go with me to the banquet Friday night?"

Carrie was speechless.

"Carrie? Do you have other plans?"

"Oh, no, Tom. Are you sure—you know—you mean—me?"

"I'm sure it'll be fun, Carrie. Honest. I just got my driver's license and Dad said I could have the car."

"But—"

"I know we'd have fun."

"O.K., Tom. Thank you."

"I'll be by at six thirty, Carrie. O.K.?"

"I'll be ready."

"Bye."

Slowly Carrie put down the telephone receiver. It couldn't be! "Mom, Dad, Toby!" she screamed.

All three of them rushed in. Dad had the newspaper in one hand, his shoes off. Mom's hands were wet from the dishwater. Toby had his shirt half off.

"What in the world?" Mom asked.

"Hey, guess what? I have a date. A real honest-to-goodness date!"

"Oh, no," Toby said disgustedly. "Big deal. Tom, no doubt! I thought you were dying or something. Excuse me!" He left.

"Mom, Tom asked me to the banquet. Dad, I have to have a new dress. Mom, will my shoes fit? Daddy, can I go just with Tom?"

"Wait, Honey. Slow down." Her dad sat down on the bed, smiling.

Mom sank into the easy chair, drying her hands on her apron. "I'm so glad, Carrie."

"Can I have a new dress? Can Tom help me? I can do almost everything myself."

"I think so, Carrie."

"Mom, I have to have my finished legs or I can't wear nylons."

"I'll check tomorrow."

"I've gotta call Janey. She won't believe it. Excuse me." Carrie grabbed the phone and dialed.

Her mom and dad left, smiling at each other.

The next day was an at-home and study day for Carrie. Her mother went shopping and brought home three dresses for Carrie to choose from. They decided to keep the pale-gold flowered one. It had a square neck, little puffed sleeves, a fitted top, and a full skirt with a ruffle on the bottom. She had to stand to see it right.

Mom said her finished legs would be ready. They would be all smooth, the bolts and screws covered with the plastic. Under nylons they would look almost real.

Her mother had surprised her with low gold shoes and a small gold bag. There was also a sparkly gold clip for her hair, which was now quite long. Mom offered to lend Carrie her brown fur jacket.

It was all so exciting! She had to call Janey to come over and see everything.

Just before she turned out her light, Daddy came in and sat on her bed.

"Carrie, I have to tell you something." He had the newspaper in his hand.

"Yes, Dad?"

"I asked them especially not to give this any publicity, but it is here anyway. Look."

Staring at her from the printed page was the face she had drawn.

"Wight, Daniel Roman," Carrie muttered.

"What, Carrie?"

"That's his name. I remember now! Wight, Daniel Roman."

"That's great. I'll call and tell the police. The sooner they pick him up, the safer we'll be!"

"What do you mean, Daddy?"

"What do you think Mr. Wight will do when he sees his picture in the paper as a wanted man? Especially after a night watchman was hurt seriously on one of their last raids."

"He won't appreciate it!"

"That's for sure. And who put him in danger?"

"Oh, oh!"

"Exactly. We have asked for protection. We will be very careful."

"The danger is to me, and Sara, and Toby. And Scraps, too."

"The paper mentioned that the drawing had been done by a fifteen-year-old. That is too much of a clue for Mr. Wight! In other words, be most alert. Report anything suspicious."

"O.K., Daddy."

"Please do not discuss this with your mother. I hope it is cleared up before we leave next Saturday. She will never go if she thinks there is any danger. She needs this vacation very much. We'll have to trust the police to take care of things."

"Can I go on my date?"

"I'm sure Tom and I can work something out."

"Thanks, Dad."

"I'm proud of you, Honey, in so many ways. I'm sure our troubles will soon be over, and you will be walking."

He gave her a hug and a kiss and hurried out before she could reply.

13

"Mom, I can't go! I've never been on a date alone before. How will I act? What will we talk about? Mom, I'm scared."

"Simmer down, Carrie. I'm giving you breakfast in bed because you will be up late tonight. Here, put on your robe."

"I just can't go. It's impossible."

"All right. I'll call Tom and tell him you are not able to go. I'm sure he will understand."

"Oh, Mom!"

"Well, you *are* being silly! He wouldn't have asked you if he didn't want you to go with him. After all, he does understand more than the rest of your friends. He was there when it all happened."

"You're right. But, but—Mom, I'm scared."

"That's normal. Any girl would be. By the way, Carrie, why is Sara hanging around so much? And Toby. Toby won't leave the house. What's the big secret?"

Carrie tried to think what to say. "Guess they're just trying to be near if you need help."

"Me? What for?"

"You and Dad are leaving tomorrow—"

"I don't need help. Been almost packed for days. I'm really

73

excited too, Carrie. But I do hate to leave you. I sure hope you can manage."

"You know I can. Shall I get up for breakfast?"

"No, Honey. I have it all ready. Guess I'm excited about my travel date, too."

She was back almost immediately with a pretty breakfast tray. There was a small package on it.

"This came in the mail addressed to you, Carrie. A surprise, I guess."

Hurrying, Carrie tore off the wrapping paper and opened the white box. Inside was a small ceramic poodle that looked just like Scraps.

"What a shame," Mother said. "Its head is broken off. Isn't it cute. I'm sure we can glue it."

"Don't touch it, Mom. Is Daddy gone yet? I've got to show him. Right away!"

"I'll see. He was just finishing his second cup of coffee." She hurried out.

Dad came at once. "I made Mom stay downstairs. What is this about a dog?"

"Look, Daddy."

"A poodle with its head broken off! I don't like this, Carrie. What did you touch?"

"Just the outer wrapping."

"Good girl. I'll take this all, just as it is, in a newspaper to the police. Evidently they haven't caught our friend Wight yet."

"Dad, I'm scared."

"No need to be. The police are on patrol. I'll alert them to this."

"That was a nasty thing to do."

"You're so right! Now leave it to me." He gathered the

74

package up and wrapped it in paper. He kissed her good-by. "I'll call you from downtown if there is any news."

Finally she was alone. Breakfast was rather cold, but it tasted good. She ate slowly. There was so much to think about. Her dress looked beautiful hanging on the closet door. No one would see her legs under that long skirt. Just her gold shoes.

Maybe she would try to stand. Maybe if they played "The Star-spangled Banner," or stood for prayer, or something. That would really surprise everyone!

She wondered how her hair looked. Moving the tray, she took the curlers out of her hair and brushed it. It looked good now, but tonight was a long time away. She put the curlers back in carefully. She knew Mom wouldn't approve of her washing it again.

The day crawled. Lessons wouldn't come right. Everything went wrong. She redid her nails. Then she began to clean the drawers in her nightstand. That got her started and she went on cleaning and straightening her dresser and desk. It took a couple of hours.

Mom tried to get her to take a nap after lunch. She watched the afternoon movie instead. It was very boring, about ancient Greek times, gods, heroes, and stuff.

Janey came right after school. They talked excitedly, and Carrie got nervous all over again. Janey promised to stay near all evening in case Carrie needed something.

Finally it was time to get ready. Mom helped her. It took quite a while to get herself all set, and even a few tears. She wheeled into Mother's room to use the full-length mirror.

"Am I O.K., Mom, really?"

"Honey, you look beautiful, believe me!"

Daddy was standing in the doorway. His eyes were soft and shiny. "Honey, you are lovely. So grown up!"

She checked to see if the brakes were set, carefully pushed up the chair's foot pieces, as she had practiced, and slowly lifted herself up. Mom steadied her. She was standing. The dress swished around her feet.

Mom had tears in her eyes.

The doorbell rang.

Carrie sat down suddenly. "It's Tom."

"Hey, Sis," Toby yelled. "Tom's here."

"Oh, that brat! Mom, make him——"

"It's all right, Carrie. I'll go down," Dad said. "You and Mom come soon."

Never in all her life would Carrie forget that evening. It went so perfectly. Tom even brought a lovely orchid! It was cream-colored with green edges. Her very first!

She knew by how Tom's face looked that he thought she was beautiful. He just swallowed and said, "Hi, Carrie."

Carrie got into the car with very little help. Tom drove carefully the two blocks to the gym. He must have prepared ahead of time, because several of the fellows were near the door to help get her chair out of the trunk, unfold it, and help push her inside.

Everyone greeted her, and several of the girls told her how pretty she looked.

It was exciting to sit at the head table with Tom, the team captain. And even more exciting when Tom was awarded his letter. The special award, a miniature gold basketball charm, he asked Carrie to keep for him. She slipped it into her gold purse.

When they all stood up at the end of the program to honor the award winners, Carrie stood too, tall and straight. Tom couldn't believe it. Much of the clapping was for her as well!

They stayed quite a while afterward. Many of the couples were dancing, but Carrie didn't even notice. There were too many things to talk about, so much news to learn. The evening went quickly.

"Carrie, I had such a good time," Tom said, as he turned the car into her driveway. "Thanks for going with me."

"You were so nice to take me," she answered. "Oh, I almost forgot. Here is your gold basketball."

"Would you like to keep it for me? Please."

"Yes, Tom. I'd like to."

"I hope we can do a lot of things together from now on," Tom said.

The outside lights were on, and Dad came to help Tom put her in the wheelchair and take her in. Mom was still up, and the four of them had a pleasant half hour in the kitchen with hot chocolate and cookies.

Tom thanked them politely and said good-by. "I'll call you," he told Carrie as he left.

"Well, Baby?" Daddy questioned.

"Oh, it was so very wonderful!" she sighed.

"How was the dinner?" Mom asked.

"Good—I don't even remember! They liked the decorations. Look what Tom let me keep for him. It was all such fun!"

"Bedtime, little lady," Daddy said, smiling, and picked her up in his strong arms. Gently he carried her upstairs to her room. Mom followed and tucked her in.

"I'll tell you all about it tomorrow, Mom. I'm so sleepy."

She had no trouble saying her prayers. There was no question. Everything was going to work out—in time.

14

CARRIE WAS ON THE SECOND HALF HOUR'S TELEPHONE CON-
versation with Janey, going over every detail of last night.

Dad came into her room and signaled for her to stop.

"Call you back," she told Janey. "What's wrong, Daddy?"

"The police insist that Mother and I not change our plans,
Carrie. They have men on patrol and they expect to pick that
fellow up at any moment."

"He got a package to me."

"That won't happen again. It is their business to protect you,
Carrie. They will go by often, and you have a phone handy.
They seem to think it is important for us not to change our
plans."

"O.K., Daddy."

"I just don't feel right about leaving you kids, but, since
Mom is so excited, and your grandparents will be here, I guess
we'll go ahead."

"Sure, Daddy. We'll be careful."

"I will call you every evening. I have written out where we
will be each day so you can contact us if you need to. Here it
is. I'll put it beside your phone. Grandma and Grandpa will be
here by six o'clock to stay for the week. Try to do as much for

yourself as you can. Let Toby help you."

"O.K., Daddy."

"We will leave right after lunch."

Carrie went downstairs and out the back door to the drive-way to tell them good-by. Mom kept talking nervously and kissing them both. Dad grumbled about all the things Mom was taking.

At the last minute Mom couldn't find her purse. She looked frantically, shouting directions to Toby. Carrie finally noticed it standing on the driveway by the open car door.

Daddy picked Mother up and put her in the front seat, and Toby placed the big heavy purse in her lap. They were all laughing and shouting.

Carrie had to hold Scraps tight in her arms. He was in and out of the car half a dozen times, barking frantically.

They were finally gone. Carrie and Toby noticed it was two o'clock by the kitchen clock. They decided they were hungry again.

Toby made a big fat peanut butter and strawberry jam sand-wich. Carrie was disgusted when Toby bit into it and the jam squished out and dripped down the front of his T-shirt. He just laughed and washed it off while the shirt was still on him.

"It'll dry. You won't even notice it. Sandwich is no good without lots of jam."

"Huh!" Carrie grunted. Her dill pickle and peanut butter tasted good, too.

They gave Scraps a piece of bread with peanut butter on it. Toby gave it a push against the top of Scraps' mouth. It was really funny watching the tiny dog's antics as he tried to get it loose to eat it. He even rolled over and over.

The phone rang. It was Sara wanting to come over. Her

mother was going shopping and she didn't want to go. Toby wasn't too anxious but Carrie invited her. She arrived immediately.

"Hey, Toby, you guys all alone? Aren't you scared?" Sara said, helping herself to bread and jam.

"Why be scared?" Toby asked scornfully.

"That man might come."

"He wouldn't dare. There are police all over the place."

"I don't see any."

"Be quiet, Sara. You're just scaring yourself. Toby, Daddy said to lock everything until Grandma and Grandpa get here." Carrie spoke to them both.

"Oh, yeah, I forgot."

Toby and Sara made the rounds of doors and windows while Carrie cleaned up. Carrie could hear them yelling at each other in the front room.

She heard the back-porch door open and close.

"Mrs. Riley?" she called. No answer.

She wheeled around.

"Hello, little lady." A tall man with a thin face and beady eyes was standing by the door. She recognized him at once. Her drawing had come to life.

"You know me, I see." It was the deep voice she had heard on the telephone. "You must be the one I owe all my troubles to," he added, staring at her stumps and the wheelchair.

She started to wheel away from him toward the dining room. He stepped in front of her.

"Just a minute, miss. Let's be careful now!"

Toby and Sara came bursting in, skidding to a stop. Scraps was frantic. He ran in circles around and around the man, barking loudly.

Toby tried to catch Scraps to hush him up. The man grabbed the dog, choking him quiet, stuffing him under his jacket.

Toby jumped at the intruder, kicking and hitting. With one hand the man took Toby by the collar and held him helpless.

"Everybody stop," Carrie shouted. "Sara, quit howling. Toby, stop! Mister, you give me my dog."

"All of you shut up and listen." His voice was angry.

They all quieted down. He took Scraps out of his jacket. The puppy shook his head, his ears flopping. He seemed to be all right they could see, but he stayed unmoving on the man's arm.

"You kids got me in trouble. You've ruined me by your snooping. I've got to get out of the state and you're going to help me."

No one said anything.

"I want money and a car. We will wait here until your folks get back. No one will look for me here. Then your dad will help me get away, or else."

"Boy, mister, are you out of luck!" Toby jeered. "My folks just left for a whole week's vacation. You wouldn't be safe anyplace that long!"

"Is that true, girl? They wouldn't leave a couple of kids alone, not when one of them is so helpless."

"He's right, Mr. Wight." Carrie felt strangely calm, not even afraid, just angry.

"You know my name?"

"Wight, Daniel Roman."

"You little snoop!" He took a step toward her. Scraps sank his tiny teeth in the man's wrist. He yelled and jumped, throwing Scraps to the floor.

81

The pup barely touched, he was up in Carrie's lap so fast! He stood there bristling.

The man was sucking on the bleeding teeth marks, glaring angrily.

Toby had disappeared. The man caught the movement, followed, and returned, dragging Toby by the arm.

"The dumb jerk pulled the phone wires right out of the wall," Toby muttered.

"O.K., boy, I'll take the keys to the other car. Get them."

Sara was whimpering. "I want to go home."

"Shut up. Boy, get those keys and any money you have around. Hurry up!"

"Do it, Toby. There is house money in the kitchen cabinet in that square tin box," Carrie said. "Mom left a lot extra for while they are gone."

The man scooped it up, not even counting it, and stuffed it into his coat pocket. "Boy," he threatened, "I need more than this. Where is your bank?" He grabbed Toby's arm and twisted it.

"Let him go," Carrie said. "I have over thirty dollars in the bottom of my jewel box. It's gift money. You can have it."

"Get it, boy, and no funny business, or your sis will get hurt."

Toby was gone only two or three minutes. He was pale and scared.

"Now the car keys, young man."

"The keys are hanging inside that cupboard by the back door," Toby said reluctantly.

"Now, listen, you kids, you and you are going with me," he pointed at Toby and Sara. "You won't be hurt if you do just as I say."

"No," Carrie said.

"Yes, little lady. I insist. No one with good legs is going to be left to run for help. Let's go."

"No," Toby yelled.

The man stepped toward Carrie. "You'll do as I say or I'll grab that measly little dog and finish him off once and for all. I'll also give that crippled sister of yours a push she won't forget."

"O.K., mister, I'll go, but, boy, will you be sorry!"

"You touch that dog and I'll—I'll—" Sara screamed, grabbing the peanut butter knife and holding it up.

"Why you little snip," the man laughed unpleasantly. "Who are you going to hurt with a dull old table knife? Now quit playing and let's go."

"Better do as he says," Carrie ordered. "Do just as he says. No one must be hurt."

"O.K., if you say." Sara sagged and walked to the door, looking red and angry.

Toby turned. "Carrie, you be careful. We'll be O.K. I'll take care of Sara. Don't worry."

Suddenly Carrie felt like crying. She hugged Scraps to her and nodded to Toby. He looked so little and helpless as the man followed them out.

Carrie didn't move. She heard the garage door go up. A car door opened and slammed. The motor started. Where were the police? The car backed out of the drive.

Then she could move! She rolled her chair out the door and down the ramp to the driveway. The car was just pulling away, going down the street past Rileys'.

15

CARRIE WHEELED INTO THE STREET AND SAT STILL, STARING as the car disappeared. What could she do? She had never felt so helpless.

Mrs. Riley had gone shopping. The neighbors on the other side were gone for the weekend. Across the street was the empty school.

Where were the police? It was so quiet. Nothing. No one in sight. She had to get help.

She started wheeling down the street. Surely someone would help her. A pay phone wouldn't do. She had no money with her.

Somebody! Please! She hit at the chair arm with her hand. Scraps huddled in her lap. If only—if only she could walk.

Toby and Sara. Don't think. Just roll. Not too fast. Stay in control. You are the only one who knows what has happened.

She got to the corner. A car passed on the cross street. She waved frantically, but evidently they didn't see her.

It was dangerous to be in the street, but someone—

Then she started to scream. "Help me. Somebody! Help."

Finally a car was coming. It couldn't be. It was! The car skidded to a stop. Daddy jumped out and ran to her.

"Carrie! What in the world? Tell me fast."

Mom ran up and hugged her.

"He came, Daddy. He took Mom's car—and Toby and Sara. Down that way."

"I'll go call the police," Mom said, taking the wiggling Scraps in her arms. "I knew something was wrong as soon as I heard the radio say that watchman had died."

"How did you know? You said you forgot your overnight case!"

Mom pointed to the backseat at her small suitcase. "I had to make an excuse. That man, I talked to him twice. He came to the house. He said he was selling typewriters. I recognized the picture in the paper."

"Mom, you didn't say anything—"

"It really didn't click until I heard that news report." She turned to her husband. "Now get going. The gas gauge was on empty. Just enough to get to the station, so he'll need another car. Look in the supermarket parking lot. It's on the way to the freeway."

"Dad, I'm going too."

"No, Carrie."

"Please, Daddy. It's all my fault."

"Carrie will be O.K. in the car. You go. Quick! Here come the police. I'll tell them," Mom urged.

Dad picked Carrie up and put her in the car. He ran around to the driver's side, and they pulled away just as a police car stopped behind them.

"That mother of yours had us all fooled," Daddy said. He put a hand over hers. "We had to come back. Both of us knew it. Did he hurt any of you, Honey?"

"Mr. Wight? No, Daddy. He threatened. He's very desperate, but he didn't seem to be real mean. Toby looked so little,

85

and Sara was so scared! Hurry, please!"

"We really don't know where we're going, Carrie. That clue of Mom's is a pretty slim one."

"I'm afraid Toby will do something foolish. He tried so hard to protect us."

"Let's hope not," Dad said. "The market is just ahead. Over there." He turned into the parking lot.

"Daddy, down there! There's Toby. And Sara!"

The two were standing by Mom's car, which was parked crosswise. Toby was jumping up and down yelling, "Help! That man is getting away. Somebody listen. Get the police!"

People weren't paying any attention. Kids play games. They just smiled and hurried on.

Dad stopped the car and jumped out. He ran to the children. Carrie started to follow. She opened the car door and swung her legs out. Then realized—she wasn't going anyplace!

Several police cars screamed up, and police poured out. They were all about half a block away down the aisle of parked cars. People were gathering. She couldn't see. How maddening. What was happening?

Even getting up on her knees didn't help. If she had her chair—or her feet! She reached over and pushed the car horn. She yelled. No one even noticed.

If Toby and Sara were here—and Mom's car—What was happening? She had to know.

"Hey, mister," she called to a man going by. "What's wrong over there?"

"Police are trying to find someone. Kidnapper, I guess. The kids are O.K. Police told us to leave."

People were moving back. The police officers were organizing. Carrie could just see Daddy's head.

"Oh," she couldn't help yelling, "I'm going to crawl down there!"

The police were searching in a pattern. The man must still be in the parking lot. They seemed to be checking each car down each row. Other police were clearing people back from the parked cars and putting up barricades. If only she could see!

There was a man in the blue car next to her. He must have been hiding. He sat there looking around. He was thin-faced with beady eyes, balding, hair wild. He saw her. He grinned widely as he recognized her.

Carrie screamed. He got out of the car and came to her. She was so helpless. If only she could run!

He lifted her out in his arms. She hit and waved her legs, screaming. It did no good. He was much too strong.

"Daddy! Help!" she screamed.

"Hold it. There he is," a police loudspeaker blared. "He has a girl. Stay back!"

"I'm leaving. Give me the car keys. No tricks!" Wight yelled.

"Hold your fire. Stand back," came the order.

Wight stood with his back to the car, Carrie shielding him. "Hold still, I don't want to hurt you," he told her. "Throw those keys, mister!"

Daddy hurried toward them.

"No closer. The keys!"

Toby yelled, "Carrie!" He tried to run to her, but his dad grabbed his arm. Sara was hiding behind them, looking white and tearful.

"Hurry up. Clear the way. I'm leaving," the man shouted.

Carrie tried to push away again. Wight squeezed her, hurting. She screamed.

Dad tossed the car keys. They fell on the ground just in front of Carrie and her kidnapper.

"Pick them up, little lady," the man ordered. He leaned over, holding her tightly. She reached down and took them. As he straightened up, a shot came sizzling under the car just missing his legs.

"Don't!" Dad yelled. "Don't fire!"

The police horn blared. "No firing. Clear the way!"

Wight backed onto the car seat, pulling Carrie with him. He put her on the seat beside him, reached across her, and closed the door. He moved into driving position and took the keys from her. He stayed hunched down as he started the car. Then they were moving, between cars, past the police, over the curb, out of the lot. He sat up, stepped on the gas, and they sped away.

16

"YOU KNOW YOU CAN'T GET AWAY," CARRIE SAID, RUBBING her arms where he had held her so tightly.

"What do you think I'm doing?"

"They know your name. They have your license number. You left Toby and Sara—"

"I didn't hurt those kids."

"No, but that guard—he died!"

The car swerved dangerously as he cut across the traffic to make a sudden turn.

"You shut up!" he growled.

She sat still, thinking. She twisted the ring on her finger around and around. She was glad she couldn't see the speed gauge. He was going much too fast. The traffic was heavy and cars were beginning to pull out of their way.

He flicked on the radio. "News alert bulletin. All cars traveling on Normandy between 58th Street and the intersection to the freeway, use extreme caution. Use alternate routes if at all possible. Police—"

He snapped it off.

She stared at him. "Just stop. Give up. You can't possibly—"

"Shut up, I said!"

Conditions were getting worse. Cars were slowing and pulling over. Several sirens could be heard. He was going much too fast.

Then Carrie knew where they were heading. Her stomach knotted. She was icily afraid. Her hands clenched, the ring biting in.

Normandy Drive made a long, smooth curve to the right, and went through a four-lane underpass under the main railroad line. Then it joined the freeway turning south. It was just ten miles to the state line.

But that curve—and that underpass! And one icy night last November! On the way to a game. They wouldn't make it this time, either. Not at this speed.

"Slow down. You must slow down. There's danger! Please!" She was crying.

Miraculously he did slow. They swept into the curve. A roadblock—just before the underpass! Police cars. Red and blue lights blinking.

Wight yelled, "Hang on!" He jerked the wheel to the left. The tires screeched, the car swayed, crossed the opposite lanes, slammed up over the curb into a planted area, and stopped.

He had the door open. He grabbed Carrie, pulled her under the steering wheel and into his arms. He ran, ducking low, up the hill, seeking cover in the shrubs.

A shot rang out and they fell. Carrie was thrown free. Wight groaned and writhed on the ground, his lower leg shattered by a carefully aimed police bullet.

Help was there immediately. "Don't move, Carrie. Are you O.K.?"

She wasn't about to move. Not yet. The accident hadn't happened. She knew she wasn't hurt. A scrape or two, and many bruises. But there had been no crashing, grinding metal. No blinding, crushing, bleeding pain. No screams. No deathly silence. No friend lying so still—who would never move again.

"Are you hurt? Girl, are you all right?"

"Yes. I'm fine." She tried to sit up, but hands held her down. A blanket was wrapped around her.

"I'm not hurt. Let me up." She had fallen on soft grass.

"You must lie still. The doctor will be here soon." A policeman was kneeling beside her, determined that she would not move.

"Carrie!" Another police car skidded to a stop. Toby, Sara, and Daddy spilled out and ran to Carrie.

"Honey, are you hurt?"

Sara was bawling loudly. Toby acted as if he was afraid to look.

Carrie laughed. She couldn't help it. Daddy grinned and held her tight.

"I'm fine. Really. My arm is scraped—but, honestly!"

"Thank God!" Daddy said.

"Make them let me up. I want to go home."

"You will have to be checked by the doctor."

"Please, Daddy, not at the hospital."

"I'll see what I can do. Toby, Sara, you make her lie still." Daddy and the policeman went down to the cars. Wight was being taken away in the police ambulance.

"Man, Sis, I was scared!" Toby kneeled down, and then sat on the grass beside her.

Sara sat close, too. "I'm so glad you aren't hurt."

"You have no idea!" Carrie began. "This is where it happened before. I was so afraid it would happen again. That my nightmare would be real again. But it didn't. I'm so thankful!"

"You mean, your feet?" Sara asked softly.

"Yes. It was icy. A big truck jackknifed in the underpass and squashed us up against the side"—her voice was low—"I was pinned in. I couldn't move. Jill was thrown out—against the wall. She—she—was killed."

"Janey's sister?"

Carrie nodded. "The others were all hurt too. Tom, Mrs. Green, Janey. But—Jill—was killed. I couldn't talk about it before. Now I can. It is finally over. Nothing can change what happened. But I know from now on—"

"You sure are brave," Toby said. He didn't notice that he was holding Carrie's hand.

"You should have seen me if I had had feet! That man wouldn't have taken you kids away from our house in the first place!"

"I believe it," Toby nodded.

"Me too," Sara said. "You're terrific, Carrie."

"No. You just do what you have to do the best you can."

An ambulance stopped just below. Daddy and the doctor came to them. Men followed with a stretcher.

"So you are Carrie Karns," the doctor said, examining her gently. "I know about you. You are quite a young lady! That arm needs dressing, and I imagine you will have quite a few bruises. And be mighty stiff. Your head doesn't hurt?"

"Not a bit, honest."

"You seem fine, Carrie, but we have to be sure. You let us take you, just for overnight."

"Daddy?"

"That would be best, Honey."

"I want to see Mother. And Scraps."

"Right. I'm sure they will let Mother stay with you. Scraps will have to wait!" Daddy said, smiling.

"Hey, she gets to ride in the ambulance," Toby fussed.

"Nothing's ever wrong with me."

The doctor was folding up his equipment. "Young man, I would say you had quite a day yourself. Kidnapped, no less. I think you and this young lady should be checked too." Carrie saw him wink at Daddy. "Everyone aboard."

Carrie was gently lifted onto a stretcher and carried to the ambulance. After they put her in, they lifted Toby and Sara in beside her.

"Have Mom bring my feet, Daddy. I'll need them," Carrie called.

The ambulance roared off, siren screeching its loudest. This time Carrie didn't mind the ride at all.

About the Author

MARJORIE COOK is a teacher-librarian, wife, mother and grandmother, and a free-lance writer.

This active author still finds time to be interested in psychology, audio-visuals, creative writing, and storytelling.

TO WALK ON TWO FEET is Mrs. Cook's first book.